THE LORD OF THE RINGS

THE FELLOWSHIP OF THE RING

VISUAL COMPANION

THE LORD OF THE RINGS

THE FELLOWSHIP OF THE RING

VISUAL COMPANION

JUDE FISHER

Houghton Mifflin Company
Boston · New York
2001

THE RINGS OF POWER

Long ago, in the Second Age of Middle-earth, there were forged nineteen Great Rings, each bestowing long life and magical powers upon the wearer. But Sauron, Dark Lord of Mordor, treacherously wrought a Ruling Ring, mixing its molten gold with his own blood and life force, by which he intended to bring all the other rings under his own control. Deep inside Mount Doom he forged it, and over it he chanted the Ring-spell which would bring it to life:

Three Rings for the Elven-kings under the sky

Seven for the Dwarf-lords in their halls of stone,

Nine for Mortal Men doomed to die

One for the Dark Lord on his dark throne

In the Land of Mordor where the Shadows lie.

One Ring to rule them all, One Ring to find them

One Ring to bring them all and in the darkness bind them

In the Land of Mordor where the Shadows lie.

The three rings held by the Elves remained untouched by his evil, and the rings of the Dwarves were safely sequestered; but the nine held by the lords of men succumbed to him and those who wore them were ensnared, condemned to walk in the permanent twilight of his Eye, reduced to the state of Ringwraiths.

THE LAST ALLIANCE OF ELVES AND MEN

In the Second Age of the Sun, Sauron cruelly enslaved the Free Peoples of Middle-earth, and his shadow stretched far over the land. Despair and fear fell across the world until a Last Alliance of Elves and Men, under the leadership of the Elven-king Gil-galad and Elendil, High King of Gondor, was forged in a desperate attempt to break his power.

On the slopes of Mount Doom, their great army drove back the Dark Lord's forces; but there Gil-galad, though as an immortal Elf-lord he was born never to die, perished beneath the heat of Sauron's hand; and Elendil fell, too, breaking beneath him his legendary greatsword Narsil, which had been forged in the First Age by the Dwarves. His son Isildur, prince of Gondor, took up the shard and with its sharp edge struck from the Dark Lord's hand the finger bearing the One Ring, thus breaking at last his will and power.

"So small a thing ..."

Then the One Ring should have been destroyed; but Isildur succumbed to its seductive power and refused to cast it away, thinking to use it for the good of his people. He carried it with him always until he fell prey to Orcs at the Gladden Fields, and there, in the great River Anduin, the Ring was once more lost.

In this way the Dark Years of the Second Age of Middle-earth ended, and the Third Age began. For thousands of years since that time, Sauron has concentrated his efforts on rebuilding his armies and on his search for the Ruling Ring. But the Ring would not lie still, and by various means has made a long, strange journey.

"He who commands the Ruling Ring ...

commands all"

1
HOBBITS

In the northwestern corner of Middle-earth lies the peaceful agricultural region known as the Shire. And in that part of the Shire called the West Farthing, beyond the East Road, is found the sleepy village of Hobbiton, a quaint rural settlement inhabited by an ancient, unobtrusive folk, known as hobbits, or "hole-dwellers." For hundreds of years they have made a good living in the rich earth of the Shire, and while the earliest of their number may well have lived in simple holes and tunnels, most now dwell in houses that have been built into the grassy hillsides – houses that are low-lying, rounded and comfortably appointed, much like the hobbits themselves, who stand barely four feet tall and like to eat as much and as often as they can. Daily hobbit meals include Breakfast, Second Breakfast, Elevenses, Luncheon, Afternoon Tea and Supper, supplemented with plenty of snacks in between. They are a cheerful, settled, well-ordered and clannish folk, priding themselves on their plenty, their ancestry and their good common sense, and are therefore most unadventurous by nature, preferring the prospect of a good smoke of pipe-weed with their feet up in front of the fire at the Green Dragon Inn to gallivanting around the world (with the notable exception of one Bilbo Baggins).

8

Hobbiton remains as inward-looking and complacent as it has been for generation on generation: a place where hobbit-folk can raise their children in safety, grow vegetables and crops, tend their flower gardens and their animals and gather mushrooms for dinner, blissfully ignorant of the dark shadows that even now are encroaching from the east, from Mordor. Although activity on the highways has increased in recent years, and strangers are more frequently seen on the outskirts of the Shire, most hobbits remain determinedly unaware that the peace they enjoy is being fiercely protected by the good offices of the wizard Gandalf (whom they associate more with fireworks than true wizardry) and the Rangers of the North. For Gandalf, the Shire represents a pocket of charm and innocence in an increasingly tainted world. Good-hearted and generous of spirit, hobbits are a folk worth saving from the horrors of the Dark Lord's rule.

BAG END

Hobbits stand less than four feet tall and their houses are equally compact and rounded; classic features of hobbit architecture include circular doors and windows, curved walls and beams. Their owners set much store by pleasant furnishings and local craftsmanship, specializing particularly in finely turned and polished wood and in skillful cabinetmaking. Hobbit holes are devoted to comfort and hospitality, containing as they do well-stocked larders, homely hearths and a ready welcome. Bilbo Baggins' house – Bag End – is a fine example of the type.

10

BILBO BAGGINS

"Far too eager and curious for a hobbit, most unnatural ..."

Scholar, poet, maker of songs, wearer of fancy brocade waistcoats, teller of stories and friend to Elves, Bilbo Baggins is one of the most famous and long-lived hobbits in the Shire's history. He is best known, however, as an adventurer, a rare thing among hobbits, following the events he has been recording in his book, *There and Back Again, A Hobbit's Tale*, in which he took part in a heroic, epic quest with Gandalf the wizard and several Dwarves, and came back to Hobbiton with a certain Ring, which he had won in a riddle contest with the creature known as Sméagol, or Gollum. Many of his neighbors – and some of his relatives – now refer to him as "mad Baggins" as a result of these adventures.

Sixty years after returning from his journey, Bilbo celebrated his eleventy-first birthday and passed all his worldly goods to his young relative Frodo, choosing instead to travel to the Elven refuge of Rivendell, there to complete his great work in tranquility and to study Elven lore in the company of Elrond Half-elven.

"The Road goes ever on and on
Down from the door where it began.
Now far ahead the Road has gone
And I must follow, if I can ..."

FRODO BAGGINS

"It is a dangerous business, Frodo, going out of your door ..."

Orphaned at a young age, Frodo Baggins was adopted by the hobbit he knows as Uncle Bilbo. Bilbo brought Frodo to live with him at his large house at Bag End, not out of charity, but because he was the only one of all his many relations to show any spirit. Frodo has grown up into a serious, sensitive and intelligent lad, fascinated by Bilbo's library and by stories of his exotic travels across Middle-earth. An apt pupil, Frodo has even learned to read and speak a little of the Elvish language, an ability that will earn him the name "Elvellon," or Elf-friend.

However, many of the inhabitants of Hobbiton are rather of the opinion that since he has spent so much time having his head turned by fanciful tales of Elves and Dwarves and dragons, Frodo is not as practical a hobbit as he should be and barely has the sense "to know a swede from a turnip," as the Shire saying goes.

Despite this, Frodo has wandered far and wide around Hobbiton, exploring the highways and byways of the Shire with his friend Sam Gamgee, and as a result has himself developed something of a taste for travel. Which is as well, since he will be called upon to undertake a long journey.

When Bilbo Baggins decides to leave Hobbiton to spend time among the Elves, he leaves not only the house at Bag End, but also the rest of his possessions, including a certain Ring, to Frodo, who must bear it out of the Shire, and way beyond.

"Even the smallest person can change the course of the future …"

Although it may look no more than a harmless gold band, the Ring is a heavy burden indeed, with its constant temptations and whisperings of Black Speech, the language of Mordor. It has the power to draw the attention of the Enemy's servants, and is the constant focus of Sauron's seeking Eye. Always the Ring wishes to return to its maker.

Whoever bears it will be in constant danger; for his protection, Frodo will receive from Bilbo an Elvish-made sword known as Sting – a magical weapon which has a blade that glows blue to warn that Orcs are close – and a mail shirt made from a marvelous substance called *mithril*, a metal mined from deep and secret places by the Dwarves. As light as a feather, but as hard as dragon scales, it can be concealed beneath clothing, yet will turn the fiercest blade. It was once given to Bilbo by the Dwarf king Thorin.

SAMWISE GAMGEE

A gardener like his father, Hamfast (known as "the Gaffer"), Sam Gamgee has spent his whole life in and around the village of Hobbiton. Although he has explored the neighboring areas of the Shire with his friends, on mushroom-gathering expeditions and vegetable-raiding forays, he has never traveled further afield, even though he has been entranced by Bilbo Baggins' exciting tales. Tending the garden at Bag End, Sam has been treated to many of Bilbo's adventure stories about his journeys to foreign parts, where he encountered the more exotic folk of Middle-earth. Elves, in particular, have taken Sam's fancy.

The barmaid at the Green Dragon Inn, Hobbiton's popular hostelry, has also captured Samwise's fancy. Young Rosie Cotton is one of the prettiest hobbits in the Shire, but unfortunately Sam is too shy to make approaches to her, despite the encouragement and teasing of his friends. Instead, he is happy to sit comfortably with a good smoke of pipe-weed and a flagon of the finest Shire ale and listen to the chatter of others.

16

Quiet, solid and dependable, Sam has always been the perfect companion for his friend and master, Frodo Baggins, to whom he is devoted. A hobbit of great heart (and great appetite), Sam refuses to be left behind when Frodo undertakes his quest, although it is not clear at the outset what skills and qualities he can bring to the quest, for while he may be a practical and loyal lad, he is neither startlingly clever, nor obviously brave, nor yet skilled with a sword.

However, adversity can make heroes of even the most unlikely folk. In Sam's case it may forge stubbornness into iron determination and fierce loyalty into extraordinary courage.

MERIADOC BRANDYBUCK

Meriadoc Brandybuck – to give him his full, and rarely used, proper name – is the son of the Master of Brandybuck and therefore comes from one of the Shire's most prominent and well-to-do families, but he is better known as Merry, an abbreviation that suits well his cheerful, sunny nature.

A mischievous, lively and audacious lad, he has long been one of Frodo Baggins' closest friends, one fond of practical jokes, pranks and getting into scrapes, particularly with his cousin Peregrin Took, more widely known as Pippin.

18

Like all hobbits, he loves to eat, drink and have fun. Mushroom-hunting, scrumping and purloining cabbages and carrots from the fields of neighboring farmers, like Farmer Maggot, and spending comfortable evenings in the bar of the Green Dragon Inn with a smoke of pipe-weed have till now been the extent of

his experience of the world, but try keeping Merry Brandybuck at home when there's an adventure to be had, especially one that may involve a little danger.

Quite how much danger he is likely to see when joining Frodo on his quest, Merry has no idea, of course, but hobbits are a surprising folk whose finest qualities come to the fore in perilous situations, and a mischievous tendency for tricks and japes may be transformed under pressure into resourcefulness and courage.

Armed with a keen-edged Elf-knife which he is given by the Ranger known as Strider, Merry is soon to discover the true meaning of the word "adventure."

PIPE-WEED

Both Pippin and Merry have a great and practical interest in one of the Shire's favorite exports: pipe-weed, a fragrant burning-herb which is smoked in long clay and wooden pipes. A common or garden variety of *Nicotiana*, pipe-weed is lovingly grown in various corners of Middle-earth, but it is generally accepted that the finest strains, including Longbottom Leaf and Old Toby, have long been propagated and developed in the South Farthing of the Shire. The habit of smoking pipe-weed has spread far and wide, from the Shire to the lands of men and beyond: Aragorn, son of Arathorn, shares the hobbits' love of the weed, as do the Istari wizards, Gandalf the Grey and Saruman the White.

PEREGRIN TOOK

"Fool of a Took ..."

Peregrin Took – known by everyone as Pippin – is the youngest of the four hobbits in the Fellowship of the Ring. Second cousin to Frodo, and cousin, too, to Merry, he has lived in the Shire for his whole life, and never set foot outside its boundaries.

Merry is his closest friend: the pair are quite inseparable, and are hardly ever seen out of one another's company. For years now they have been a menace to the inhabitants of Hobbiton and its surroundings, with their high spirits and practical jokes. Events such as Bilbo Baggins' eleventy-first birthday party, with its abundance of ale and fireworks, afford plenty of opportunities for getting into trouble.

20

If truth be told, though, Pippin is rarely the instigator in these mishaps, but tends to follow Merry's lead unquestioningly. Naive, sweet-natured and more than a little foolish, Pippin is probably the least prepared of all Frodo's companions for the danger and the darkness they are to meet on their quest. But hobbits are an adaptable, stout-hearted and determined folk, and while at the outset Pippin may prove to be rather more of a liability than an asset to the Fellowship, he will soon have the use of an Elf-sword and the need to use it in his own defense and that of his friends; and use it he will.

HOBBITS' FEET

Hobbits rarely, if ever, wear shoes or boots, and as a result they have developed feet with thick, leathery soles and furry uppers to keep out the cold.

2
MEN

"Men: they are weak. The noble blood of Númenor no longer flows
in their veins. They heed nothing but their own petty desires."

In the Second Age of Middle-earth, Elendil – High King of Gondor – and his son, Isildur, joined forces with the Elves, under the leadership of the legendary Elven-king Gil-galad, to challenge Sauron and the forces of shadow. The Battle of Dagorlad was the bloodiest of conflicts and saw the loss of both Gil-galad and Elendil, but finally the Dark Lord was driven all the way back to the slopes of Mount Doom, and there men and Elves, fighting together for the last time, brought about his fall.

With the broken blade of his father's great-sword, Narsil, Isildur – now himself the High King of men – cut from Sauron's hand the Ruling Ring, which severed him from his supernatural power; and thus the Second Age came to an end.

> *"There is weakness, there is frailty;*
> *but there is courage also, and honor*
> *to be found in men."*

Then should the Dark Lord have been laid low for all time. But men are by their very nature flawed. Instead of destroying the One Ring, Isildur desperately coveted it and decided to keep it for his own use and for the good of his kingdom, declaring that it should henceforth be the heirloom of Gondor and that all those of his bloodline should be bound to its fate. And so it is that three thousand years later, in the Third Age of Middle-earth, his descendant Aragorn, son of Arathorn, last chief of the Dúnedain and heir to the Gondorian kingdom, is to find his own destiny tied to the fate of the Ring and the quest to destroy it.

Isildur fell to an attack of Orcs at the Gladden Fields, and the Ring was lost into the waters of the Anduin. With his death, the race of men was left kingless, and since that time has dwindled and split into different factions and tribes: the Easterlings and Haradrim, who now support the Dark Lord; the Rohirrim, who dwell in the grasslands and mountains bordering Fangorn Forest, and the Gondorians, whose capital is the White City of Minas Tirith, closest of all kingdoms to the shadow of Mordor. Never since the fall of Isildur have the people of Gondor taken another king.

> *"The blood of Númenor is all but spent,*
> *its pride and dignity forgotten.*
> *Men are scattered, divided, leaderless ..."*

BREE

On the eastern border of the Shire, at the crossing of the Great East Road and the North Road, is the town of Bree. This cluster of two-storied, half-timbered stone houses lies nestled against a low wooded hill, and is the home to a motley collection of folk, its inhabitants encompassing both men and hobbits, and even one or two Dwarves. Even more folk enter the town, because of its location at the meeting of two great roads. Because of this strategic position Bree is surrounded by a thick hedge, and a great gate manned by a gatekeeper guards each entrance and exit of the Great East Road.

The favorite meeting place in the town is the famous Prancing Pony Inn, the area's most ancient public house, where travelers stop for lodgings and refreshment to break their journeys and exchange news and gossip from all over Middle-earth. The innkeeper is one Barliman Butterbur, who serves a fine pint of ale, but unfortunately has a less than fine memory.

25

ARAGORN

"One of them Rangers. Dangerous folk, they are, wandering the Wilds ..."

A tall, weather-beaten man with watchful eyes, well armed and wrapped in travel-stained clothes, is encountered by the hobbits in the Prancing Pony, the inn at Bree. Barliman Butterbur, the innkeeper, informs them that the man is called Strider, and that he is a Ranger – one of the wandering Northern men – who walk about on their long shanks, turning up from time to time, when folk least expect to see them.

Strider has a dark and dangerous look to him, but he is far more than he at first appears. In evil times, disguise and subterfuge are necessary to ward off the Enemy's eye, and Strider is soon revealed to be a close ally of Gandalf the Grey, and more besides . . .

The mysterious Strider has the noblest of heritages, for his true name is Aragorn, son of Arathorn, and he is Chief of the Dúnedain, the last remnant in the North of the ancient race of men; and although yet he wears no crown, he is a descendant of the High Kings, the heir to Isildur of Gondor. As a token of his heritage, he bears two ancient and powerful heirlooms: the broken hilt of Narsil, with which Isildur cut the One Ring from Sauron's hand; and the Ring of Barahir, a ring fashioned in the form of twin serpents with emeralds for eyes, their heads meeting beneath golden flowers which one devours and the other upholds.

Orphaned as a child, Aragorn has been raised in the house of Elrond Half-elven in Rivendell, and has long loved Elrond's daughter, the beautiful Arwen Evenstar; but she is of the long-lived Elven race and he a mortal man, and their future together requires that a terrible choice be made.

Destiny weighs heavily upon Aragorn. As a member of the Fellowship of the Ring, pledged to the service of the Ringbearer, he faces a long quest and a great war, upon which the future of the Free Peoples of Middle-earth depends. Aragorn, son of Arathorn, has a crucial and unenviable duty to fulfill in both before he can even begin to consider his own concerns.

27

BOROMIR

"Gondor has no king, Gondor does not need a king ..."

Boromir is the eldest son of Denethor, the current Steward of Gondor, who holds the high seat of Minas Tirith, the capital city of Gondor. Since the fall of Isildur, son of Elendil, at the Gladden Fields, the Gondorians have taken no king, instead appointing a noble steward to govern the country until the day when the legendary Heir of Isildur may return to claim his throne. Indeed, they have been kingless for so long now that there is no longer any expectation that such a man may exist.

"In a dream I saw the eastern sky grow dark, but in the west, a pale light lingered.

A voice was crying:'Your doom is at hand: Isildur's Bane is found!'"

28

Boromir has traveled north to Rivendell to seek the meaning of a recurrent dream which told of the waking of "Isildur's Bane" – the thing that caused the High King's death. He will learn in Rivendell that this is the One Ring, now in the possession of Frodo Baggins. Gondor lies closest of all the kingdoms of Middle-earth to the shadow: the dark peaks of Mordor are clearly visible from the battlements of Minas Tirith, and Gondorian warriors have perpetually had to fight off incursions of Orcs and other of the Dark Lord's fell creatures.

Like the ancient High King, Isildur, Boromir can also see a use for the One Ring in the defense of his people; yet when the dark, disheveled man known as Strider is revealed in Rivendell to be Aragorn, son of Arathorn, last chief of the Dúnedain and heir to the Gondorian kingdom, Boromir is not fully convinced that he is indeed the man destined to reunite the ancient kingdoms and lead them into a new age.

Despite all his doubts, he still offers his services to the Ringbearer to aid him in his quest, and becomes a valiant member of the Fellowship of the Ring.

Boromir bears with him a greatsword, his shield and the horn of a wild ox, bound with silver and inscribed with ancient letters. It is told that if this horn is blown in dire need anywhere within the boundaries of Gondor, help shall at once be sent to he who blows it; but when Boromir is hard pressed by Orcs, as the Fellowship travels south, he may be too far beyond the bounds of his homeland for help to arrive in time.

3

ELVES

"They live in both worlds at once – the Seen and the Unseen"

The fairest and oldest of all the races of Middle-earth, the Elves are possessed of great magic and the ability to create things of immense beauty, craft and enchantment – including the Rings of Power, weaponry, music, language and lore. Immortal and ageless, they have lived in Middle-earth since the earliest days and were the first of the speaking peoples of the world. But now in the Third Age a great sadness has come upon them, for their time in the world is coming to an end. Elves are now rarely seen in Middle-earth, for many of their number have already passed over the Sea to the Undying Lands, where they may continue to live forever in bliss, away from the cares and trials of a war-torn world.

"Young and old at the same time . . . so alive, but so sad"

Yet small communities of Elves still survive in the world: in Northern Mirkwood, the great greenwood; at Rivendell, their ancient refuge; and in Lothlórien, the Golden Wood, which is the province of the Lady Galadriel and Lord Celeborn. Tall and slender, keen of eye and mellifluous of speech, Elves have always walked lightly upon the earth. Their songs echo down the ages.

Nai tiruvantel ar varyuvantel i Valar tielyanna nu vilya
May the Valar protect you on your path under the sky

RIVENDELL

"There's magic here, right down deep, where you can't
lay your hands on it"

R ivendell has stood for thousands of years as a last haven and hidden refuge protected against all evil things by the power of the Elves. It lies in a deeply riven valley in eastern Eriador, in the foothills of the towering, snow-capped Misty Mountains. There, within sunlit gardens, terraces and courtyards, nestles a cluster of elegant Elven buildings, ornately carved and decorated with statues, wall paintings and fine tapestries.

Its master is Elrond, lord among Elves, and it is in Rivendell that the Council of Elrond is held, to discuss the matter of the One Ring and how it may be destroyed.

ELROND

It was during the war against Sauron in the Second Age that Elrond founded the haven of Rivendell as a safe refuge for his people, and he has been its lord ever since that time. He fought in the Battle of Dagorlad in the Last Alliance of Elves and Men, serving as herald to the Elven-king Gil-galad, who fell in that great battle. When Isildur cut the One Ring from Sauron's hand, it was Elrond who urged him to destroy the Ring in the Cracks of Doom, but his wisdom went unheeded, and instead of being destroyed for all time, Sauron was given yet another chance to rebuild his powers.

Millennia old, Elrond Half-elven is the son of Eärendil the Mariner and Elwing. He is a legendary healer and the guardian of a vast store of Elven lore. He is also the bearer of Vilya, the Ring of Air, one of the three great Elven rings that were forged in the Second Age of Middle-earth. His name – Half-elven – derives from his ancestry, for he can trace his line directly back to the hero Beren – a mortal man – and Lúthien, the Elven princess who, out of her great love for Beren, gave up her immortality to live out her days with him in Middle-earth, instead of taking passage to the Undying Lands.

It is Elrond who calls for a Council at Rivendell between representatives of all the Free Peoples of Middle-earth, to decide what is to be done with Sauron's Ruling Ring.

Elrond Half-elven's daughter is the beautiful Arwen, and he also raised the heir of the Dúnedain – Aragorn, son of Arathorn – under his protection at the Elven refuge, against the day when Aragorn might claim his rightful inheritance.

33

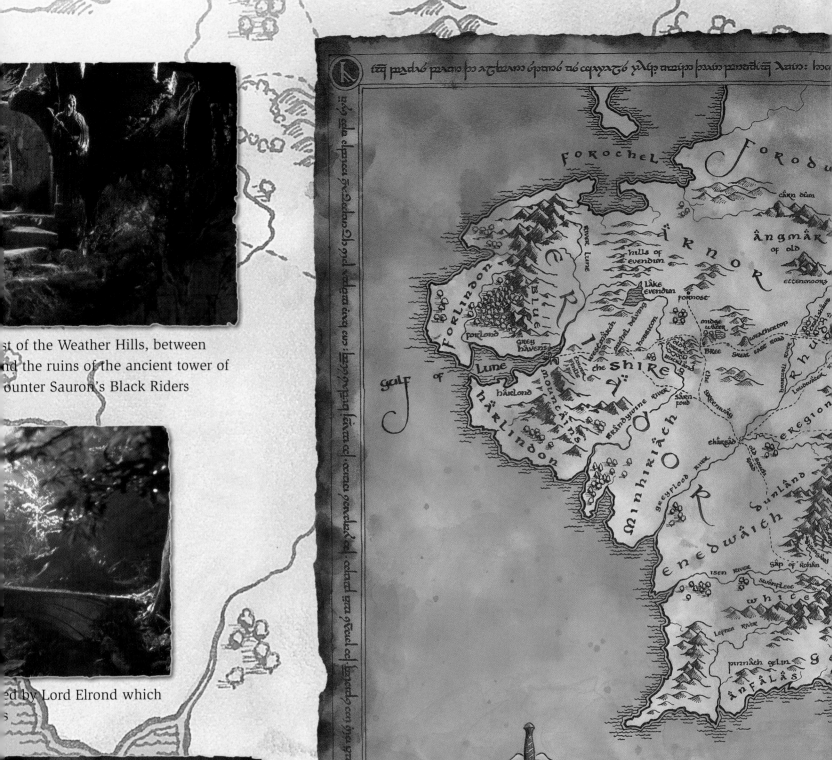

...st of the Weather Hills, between ...nd the ruins of the ancient tower of ...ounter Sauron's Black Riders

...ed by Lord Elrond which ...s

...as Moria, the greatest of the Dwarf-halls, ...eath the Misty Mountains

HOBBITON A pretty rural village in the Shire, to the northwest of Middle-earth, which is home to Bilbo and Frodo Baggins

WEATHERTOP The southernmo
Bree and Rivendell, on which sta
Amon Sûl, where the hobbits end

BREE A town of men and hobbits, situated on a crossing of two great roads on the way east out of the Shire

RIVENDELL The Elven refuge found
lies at the foot of the Misty Mountain

THE MISTY MOUNTAINS The towering mountain range that runs like a great spine from the frozen Northern Waste to the Gap of Rohan

KHAZAD-DÛM Also known
carved deep into the rock ben

ARWEN

Daughter to Elrond and granddaughter to Galadriel, Lady of the Golden Wood, Arwen is famed as the most beautiful of all living things. Her hair is dark as a river at night, her eyes of an unearthly blue. She is millennia old and, like her father, is filled with the wisdom of the ages and the lore of the Elves; yet she loves a mortal man. She was raised by the Elves of Lothlórien, the Golden Wood, but when she returned to her father's domain, she there met and fell in love with Aragorn, son of Arathorn, whom Elrond had raised since a boy, following the loss of Aragorn's parents. Now she will be faced with a terrible choice: to act according to Aragorn's will and leave with the other Elves to pass over the Sea into the Undying Lands or, like her ancestress Lúthien, to give up her death-less future and become his mortal wife.

"The light of the Evenstar does not wax and wane: it is constant, even in the greatest darkness"

Arwen wears the great and magical Elven jewel called the Evenstar (a name by which she is also often known). It symbolizes not only her goodness and beauty, but also her longevity, so in giving it to Aragorn to wear on his great journey into shadow, she gives him also her heart, and her life.

"I will bind myself to you, Aragorn of the Dúnedain: for you I will forsake the immortal life of my people."

NORTHERN WASTE

GREY MOUNTAINS

mount gundabad

withered heath

IRON HILLS

erebor

esgaroth

mountains of mirkwood

RhovÃnion

old forest road

RhÛn

gladden

gladden fields

moria

lothlorien

lÓrien

Anduin, the great river

SEA OF RHÛn

fangorn

limlight

wold

the brown lands

west emnet

east emnet

Rohan

helm's deep

edoras

entwash

emyn muil

dead marshes

dagorlad

morannon

ÂSH MOUNTAINS

udûn

mount doom

barÂd-dûr

isengard

sorgoroch

gorgoroch

MORDOR

nurn

SEA OF NURNÉn

belfalas

lebennin

mountains of shadow

harondor

poros river

ithilien

the harad road

KHÂnd

near hÅrÅd

haradwaith

city of the corsairs

Åvens tumbÅr

fÅr hÅrÅd

LOTHLÓRIEN The Elven woo
River Anduin, ruled by Lord C

EDORAS The capital of
the horse-lords, which li
and Gondor

MINAS TIRITH The seven-level
dom of Gondor in the south of M
the lands of Mordor

...land realm west of the
...leborn and Lady Galadriel

RIVER ANDUIN The great river which flows from the Grey
Mountains in the north to the Bay of Belfalas in the south

...Rohan, kingdom of
...es between Eriador

ISENGARD The impregnable fortress which guards the Gap of
Rohan and is occupied by the wizard Saruman the White

...ed chief city of the king-
...iddle-earth, bordering

MORDOR The dread realm of the Dark Lord, Sauron, in the far southeast
of Middle-earth

LEGOLAS

Prince Legolas – whose name in Elvish means "Greenleaf" – is the son of King Thranduil of the Woodland Realm. He has traveled south to Elrond's Council at Rivendell to act as the envoy of the Woodland Elves who inhabit the great northern forest of Mirkwood. This once-beautiful forest is even now being overrun by Orcs, wolves and other dark, wandering spirits in thrall to the powers of darkness as the shadow of Mordor stretches ever further across Middle-earth.

The Elves being a long-lived race, Legolas knows the Ranger Strider of old and is well aware of his true identity. Like many of his people, he has a distrust of Dwarves, which will result in a prickly relationship with the envoy of the Dwarves of Erebor, Gimli, son of Glóin.

Legolas brings a number of unique and beneficial skills to the Fellowship of the Ring – the brother-hood of Nine Walkers chosen by Elrond to bear the Ring across Middle-earth. Elves have the preternatural ability to move more lightly across the ground than the other peoples of Middle-earth; Legolas is able to run swiftly and effortlessly across the roughest terrain, barely leaving footprints even upon new-fallen snow. As a forest Elf, he is a master of woodcraft, able to scan his environment in order to read even the most minute traces and tracks left by the birds and beasts of the world. He can also see with greater clarity and over longer distances than the rest of the Nine Walkers, and is a superb and deadly shot with an Elvish longbow, which he pledges in Frodo Baggins' service.

Legolas also carries two Elf-knives: long white knives with filigreed blades – deadly weapons, for the Elves make the keenest of all blades in Middle-earth.

43

LOTHLÓRIEN

"The strange magic of the Golden Wood ..."

Just east of the Misty Mountains, beside the Silverlode, which flows into the Great River Anduin, lies Lothlórien – the Golden Wood – the fairest Elf-kingdom remaining in Middle-earth.

Lothlórien is home to the Wood Elves, who are almost invisible to visitors to the wood they guard, as they move swiftly and silently through the tree canopy, camouflaged by their magical gray cloaks. Throughout the Golden Wood grow the towering mallorn trees, the tallest and most beautiful trees in Middle-earth.

In the grass of the forest floor bloom the golden stars of elanor and pale white flowers of the niphredil. The silver pillars of the mallorns tower up into a splendid canopy of golden leaves, in the many-leveled branches of which the Elves build their flets: their dwellings, or high houses.

"The heart of Elvendom on Earth ..."

At the heart of the Golden Wood lies Caras Galadhon, the city in which the Lord Celeborn and Lady Galadriel have their royal hall, a magnificent flet nestled high in the crown of the mightiest mallorn of all.

THE LADY GALADRIEL

The Lady Galadriel – "lady of light" – grandmother of the Lady Arwen, is an Elven queen of extraordinary beauty, with her timeless features and golden river of hair. She is, however, no mere fey being, but a lady of great power. She bears one of the Great Rings – Nenya, the Ring of Adamant – and with the One Ring in her grasp as well, she would be a mighty match for the Dark Lord, Sauron.

"The mirror shows many things – things that were, things that are and things that might not yet have come to pass"

46

Galadriel also possesses a magical mirror in which those invited to look may see images of the past, present or future when determining a course of action.

Her husband is the Lord Celeborn, who comes originally from the northern kingdom of Mirkwood. His hair is long and silver and his face grave and handsome, showing little sign of his great age.

Lord Celeborn and Lady Galadriel have kept the Golden Wood as a safe haven for those Elves who have chosen to remain in Middle-earth rather than take ship to the Undying Lands, through magical means and by the vigilant care of their warriors, led by such captains as the Wood-Elf Haldir.

Galadriel and Celeborn make many wondrous gifts to the Fellowship, including Elven cloaks, which will make them all but invisible to the eyes of their enemies, fastened by brooches fashioned like leaves in silver and green; wafers of lembas, Elvish waybread (though apparently insubstantial, a single bite will sustain a full-grown man); three Elven boats, so that they can make passage down the River Anduin rather than through Orc-ridden lands; an ornate Elvish hunting knife to Aragorn; a longbow and an exquisitely tooled quiver of arrows to Legolas; silver belts and small silver daggers to Merry and Pippin; a coil of rope made from magical *hithlain* to Sam, which may serve him better than any sword; and for Frodo a crystal vial containing the light of the legendary Eärendil, which will light the darkest places when all other lights go out.

4

DWARVES

One of the most ancient and long-lived of the Free Peoples of Middle-earth are the Dwarves, a tough, stout folk who stand shorter than men but taller than hobbits, and inhabit the hidden places of the world in huge underground cave systems and tunnel complexes.

Dwarves are famed for their great prowess in battle, and for their legendary skills in mining and working with both metal and stone. From time immemorial they have crafted extraordinary artefacts in their smithies – the finest axes, swords and jewelry – and created monumental architecture far beneath the earth. Mining deep into the roots of the mountains to extract precious metals and jewels, they came upon the marvelous substance known as mithril – a beautiful silver metal which runs in deep veins through the vast, majestic Dwarven kingdom of Moria, or the Black Chasm, which is called in their language Khazad-dûm. Mithril has remarkable properties, being both incredibly hard and amazingly light, and is therefore highly prized. The Dwarves' love of such riches has gained them a reputation, fairly or unfairly, for gold-hunger and greed.

Following the war between Sauron and the Elves in the Second Age, the Dwarves of Moria retreated from the conflict into their mountain kingdom and closed their doors on the world, so where before there was trade and friendship between the Elves and the Dwarves, there has since been mistrust and even hostility between the two races.

GIMLI

"I've known him since he was knee-high to a hobbit"

One of the noble Dwarves of Erebor, the Lonely Mountain, Gimli, son of Glóin, has been sent as an envoy to the Council of Elrond in Rivendell, where he is to represent his people in the matter of the Ring. There he will volunteer to be one of the Nine Walkers to accompany Frodo on his quest.

Like all Dwarves, Gimli is both stubborn and tough, proud and indomitable, and a mighty warrior. He can also be bad-tempered and cantankerous, and like many of his kin has a deep-seated mistrust of Elves and their strange and sorcerous ways.

51

Nevertheless, he will pledge his axe in Frodo's service, and even try to bear with reasonably good grace the company of an Elf among the Fellowship.

As befits a great warrior, Gimli wears full armor – a heavy mail shirt, leather armor and an ornate Dwarvish helmet. He also carries a number of weapons: a tall walking-axe of Ereborian design, with its crescent-mooned blade; two throwing-axes – one a smaller version of the walking-axe, the other a hatchet; and in Khazad-dûm, he will avail himself of a mighty double-headed battle-axe, the epitome of traditional Morian design, as denoted by its powerful, straight and blocky blades.

MORIA

"Their own masters cannot find them if their secret is forgotten …"

In order to enter the underground Dwarven kingdom of Moria from the old Elven road from Hollin, it is necessary to locate and open one of the invisible gates in the rock. In older times, such doors stood open and were guarded by a doorwarden, but in the Third Age, such days of trust have long passed. If one who knows the secret passes his hands over the rock, pale silver patterns will be revealed, patterns that will glimmer in the light of the Moon; such symbols as the emblems of Durin, Lord of Moria (a hammer and anvil), a crown and seven stars, two trees surmounted by crescent moons, and a single star (the Star of the House of Fëanor) will all shine out.

These symbols have been made of *ithildin* (Elvish for "starmoon"), a substance that mirrors only moonlight and starlight and will disclose itself solely to someone who can speak the ancient languages of Middle-earth.

The inscription on the door is written in an old form of Elvish, and reads: "The Doors of Durin, Lord of Moria. Speak, friend, and enter."

MITHRIL SILVER

"The wealth of Moria was not in gold or jewels, but mithril …"

Only in the deepest mines of Moria, in the roots of the mountains, was this precious substance found. Other names for it are Moria silver and true silver. Its Elvish name is mithril. It was prized more highly than gold, and from it the Dwarves made a metal that was remarkably hard, yet wondrously light. Frodo has inherited a mail shirt of mithril silver from Bilbo, which had been a gift from the Dwarf king Thorin.

THE ISTARI

The word "Istari" is an Elvish term denoting an order or brotherhood of wizards.

Such wizards are Maiar – spirits older than Middle-earth itself – who have been sent by the Valar, the oldest and greatest beings of all – out of the Undying Lands into the mortal world to guide the Free Peoples of Middle-earth in their fight against the growing evil of the Dark Lord, Sauron. They have come secretly, limited to the forms of men and to those powers found only within Middle-earth. They may be known by their tall hats, long robes and the strange staffs they carry.

Each of the Istari is distinguished by a specific color, denoting his power and rank in the order: thus Saruman, highest of the Istari, is known as "the White" and wears flowing white robes, while Gandalf the Grey begins his journey through Middle-earth as a wizard of lesser power.

GANDALF THE GREY

"It's that wandering conjuror, Gandalf ..."

Being fond of the race of hobbits, the wizard Gandalf visits Hobbiton from time to time, to see his friend Bilbo Baggins (with whom he has shared many adventures) and to oversee the safety of the Shire and ensure the shadow that stretches ever further from Mordor does not encroach upon this delightfully sleepy rural backwater.

But to the inhabitants of Hobbiton he is known largely as a wandering conjuror, a blower of smoke rings and purveyor of fireworks. Little do the small folk realize the true powers of their occasional visitor. They see only his outward form: that of an old graybeard robed in a dusty cloak with a tall, pointed hat upon his head, a man worn by the passage of time, who uses his staff as a mere walking stick, to lean upon and aid his travel.

"Why did the Valar send me here in this old man's body, prone to every

mortal ache and pain?"

As one of the Istari, Gandalf is able to wield potent magic, and is immensely knowledgeable about Middle-earth's history and the lore of its many peoples. His true age is unknown.

It is Gandalf the Grey, known by the Elves as Mithrandir, who will lead the Fellowship out of Rivendell at the beginning of their quest to destroy the Ruling Ring in the fires of Mount Doom, although the temptation to use the Ring himself must surely be strong. Even though his instinct would be to use it to good purpose, Gandalf knows that the power of the Ring added to his own innate strength would create a force too great and terrible to imagine.

To do battle with the forces of darkness, Gandalf the Grey can call upon not only his spellcraft, but also his staff of power, and the Elven sword Glamdring.

"It is not the strength of the body that matters, but the strength of the spirit."

SARUMAN THE WHITE

"The wisest of my Order: his knowledge of Ring-lore is deep.

Long has he studied the arts of the Enemy."

The wizard Saruman the White, Lord of Isengard, is the greatest of the Istari brotherhood, known throughout Middle-earth for his vast store of knowledge of all things arcane and esoteric. He has devoted much study to the matter of the Rings of Power and in particular to the Ruling Ring – its making and its history as it has passed from one hand to another, and into obscurity – believing that if he and his Order find it, they themselves can make the best use of it against the growing power of the Dark Lord.

"The world is changed, Gandalf. A new age is at hand: the Age of Men,

which we must rule. Are we not the Istari? Within this frail human form does not

the spirit of a Maia live?"

Saruman's home is Orthanc, a vast tower hewn from a solid pillar of unbreakable black obsidian which rises to a great pronged spire. The Tower of Orthanc stands at the heart of Isengard, the strategic fortress that lies in a commanding position between the Misty Mountains and the Gap of Rohan. Its main defense is a natural ringwall of stone that measures a mile or more from rim to rim, enclosing beautiful trees and gardens, watered by streams that flow down from the mountains. Unknown to all but Saruman, Isengard is home to one of the rare seeing-stones, the palantír, a great ball of black stone with which the wizard is able to spy upon the whereabouts and fortunes of both allies and foes throughout Middle-earth.

"Creation is the greatest power"

The caverns below Isengard hide another secret. Down there, a new breed of creature is being hatched, as Saruman plans to form an army of his own to rival the Dark Lord's . . .

THE DARK POWERS

"The Enemy has many spies in his service, many ways of hearing . . .
even birds and beasts . . ."

Since his fall at the Battle of Dagorlad, Sauron has been regrouping his forces, even though he has failed to find again the Ruling Ring which he so treacherously forged and which was taken from him by Isildur, the High King of Gondor, and then lost, seemingly forever.

In the millennia that have passed since his fall he has slowly but inexorably increased his great army of fell beings and rebuilt his fortress at Barad-dûr. His powers are now so strong that if he can lay his hands upon the One Ring once more he will be able to break down all resistance in Middle-earth and cover all the lands in a second darkness.

His Eye ever seeks his Ruling Ring, and he has many servants upon whom to call as his spies and soldiery. The greatest and most fearsome of these are his Nazgûl, known also as the Ringwraiths; but the forces of darkness include many fell creatures, such as Orcs and Uruk-hai, Trolls and Wargs and other monsters.

ORCS

"They were once Elves..."

Orcs are not a natural part of Middle-earth, for they were originally created by the Dark Powers. Long ago, in the First Age, Elves were taken captive, tortured and mutilated in the dungeons of the Dark Lord, until they had been transformed from the most beautiful and noble of the world's folk into a ruined and terrible new form of life: Orcs. These creatures multiplied until the Dark Lord had grown himself a monstrous army with which to oppress the Free Peoples of the world. Filled with his dark will, they are swarthy and stunted, vicious and evil, and bear little relation to their noble Elven ancestors. Bred in darkness, they hate the light, and when they issue out to do their master's will, it is with demonic energy and cruel blades.

Now, in the Third Age, their kind has spawned such multitudes that they range widely across the world, and are often to be seen as far west as Mirkwood and the edges of the Golden Wood of Lothlórien, a province sacred to the Elves. Others have colonized the great Dwarf-halls of Khazad-dûm.

The foulness of their looks and ferocity of their behavior is matched by the ugliness of their language, which, although a degraded form of Westron, the native language of Middle-earth, has in the mouths of the Orcs taken on a vile sound, tainted further by the introduction of words and phrases of the guttural Black Speech of Mordor, whence they originate.

MORIA ORCS

After the Dwarves had abandoned the city of Moria, their ancient home beneath the Misty Mountains, Orcs moved in to occupy the vast halls and passages that were thus left uninhabited. The Orcs of Moria have developed dark skin and pale, protuberant eyes in response to their underground environment, where they scuttle about like insects, using the spikes on their black armor to aid them in their movement up and down the walls and pillars of Khazad-dûm.

URUK-HAI

"Seldom do Orcs journey in the open, under the Sun –
yet these have done so"

Beneath the citadel of Isengard, in the caverns deep beneath its tower, the wizard Saruman has been breeding his own race of super-Orcs – an army to rival that of Sauron, the Dark Lord. By crossing Orcs with Goblin-men, he has created a race of creatures of unparalleled power and brutality. These are the Uruk-hai: taller and straighter than men, massively muscled, black-blooded and lynx-eyed. Tireless and considerably more intelligent and powerful than the Moria Orcs, they are a fearsome fighting breed, with their viciously efficient straight-bladed weapons and long-range bows. Led by Lurtz, the Uruk-hai of Isengard are easily identifiable by the mark of the White Hand of Saruman which they bear in battle.

THE NAZGÛL

THE NINE SERVANTS OF SAURON

The Nazgûl were once great kings of men to whom Sauron gave nine of the Rings of Power and with them the promise of eternal life and dominion. They took the Rings without question, but their greed blinded them to the Dark Lord's true nature and likely treachery: one by one they fell under the power of the Rings, their bodies and souls corrupted by the Dark Lord's evil, until at last they ceased to be human and became instead insubstantial wraiths. Faceless and formless, they have been worn away to terrifying ghouls, shrouded in black robes and armor.

Mounted upon their vast, black, flame-eyed steeds, they are known as the Black Riders. Their weapons are not merely swords of steel and flame, nor their maces and morgul-daggers, which carry a deadly poison; their Black Breath also infects with despair and terror all those who are touched by it. No weapons can harm them except for those made by the Elves, and any blade that strikes them will perish.

Recently they have been seen in the vicinity of the Shire.